YES YOU!

First published in 1993
by Hodder Children's Books.
This edition published in 2007

Copyright © Mick Inkpen 1993

Hodder Children's Books
338 Euston Road, London, NW1 3BH

Hodder Children's Books Australia
Level 17/207 Kent Street, Sydney, NSW 2000

The right of Mick Inkpen to be identified as the author
and illustrator of this Work has been asserted by him in
accordance with the Copyright, Designs and Patents Act 1988.

A catalogue record of this book is available
from the British Library.

ISBN: 978 0 340 93108 0
10 9 8 7 6 5 4 3

Printed in China

Hodder Children's Books is a division of
Hachette Children's Books.
An Hachette Livre UK Company
www.hachettelivre.co.uk

Lullabyhullaballoo!

Mick Inkpen

Hodder
Children's
Books

A division of Hachette Children's Books

The sun is down.
The moon is up.
It is bedtime for the
Little Princess.
But outside the castle…

A dragon is roaring.
What shall we do?
He's hissing and snorting!
What shall we do?
We'll tell him to SSSH!
That's what we'll do.

SSSH!

But,

The brave knights are clanking.

What shall we do?

They're rattling and clunking!

What shall we do?

We'll tell them to SSSH!

That's what we'll do.

SSSH!

YES YOU!

But,
The ghosts are oooooing.
What shall we do?
They're ooo ooo oooooing!
What shall we do?
We'll tell them to SSSH!
That's what we'll do.

SSSH!

YES YOOOOOOOOU!

B{.ut,}

The giant is stamping.

What shall we do?

He's galumphing and stomping!

What shall we do?

We'll tell him to SSSH!

That's what we'll do.

SSSH!

Yes do!

But,
Out in the forest,
   Wolves are howling,
Owls are hooting,
   Frogs are croaking,
Mice are squeaking,
   Bats are flapping,
Bears are growling.

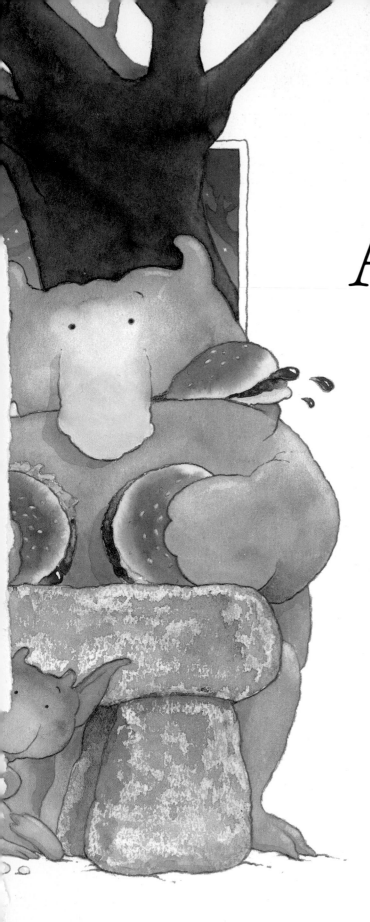

And the trolls
and the goblins
are guzzling
and gobbling
and slurping
and burping!

What shall we do?

We'll tell them to…

...STOP!

But now,
The Princess is crying!
What shall we do?
She won't stop howling!
What shall we do?
We'll sing her a lullaby.
That's what we'll do.
We'll ALL sing a lullaby.

Now the Princess is smiling.

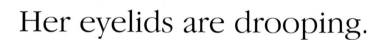

Her eyelids are drooping.

The Princess is sleeping.

So what shall we do?
We'll tiptoe to bed.
And we shall sleep too.
We shall sleep too.

But,

snore!

snore!

snore!

snore!

snore!

snore!

Snore!

...the Princess is snoring!
What *shall* we do?

S

snore!

snore!